A. E. Bennett

Footprints of a Pilgrim

in the whatsoever-walk

A. E. Bennett

Footprints of a Pilgrim
in the whatsoever-walk

ISBN/EAN: 9783337291273

Printed in Europe, USA, Canada, Australia, Japan

Cover: Foto ©Andreas Hilbeck / pixelio.de

More available books at **www.hansebooks.com**

FOOTPRINTS

OF A PILGRIM

IN THE

Whatsoever-Walk.

BY

Mrs. A. E. Bennett.

PHILADELPHIA:
George W. McCalla.
1895.

PREFACE.

IT is with feelings of abasement that I come before the public in this capacity. I have long felt that sometime I should record in a consecutive way God's gracious dealings with me. How, or in what way, I knew not, and so left it, with the feeling, that if it was Divinely ordered, it would be brought about in His way. Still my friends often urged that I thus take up my pen.

But under the pressure of cares and "labors more abundant," I saw no way of so doing, nor could I until it was given me.

When God's time came it was in such an unlooked for way, that I recoiled wholly from it. The publisher of this little work wrote to me, asking permission to use some of my articles

previously given to the public. At
first I felt I could not allow my little
writings to come thus before the public. But as I devoutly laid the matter
before the Lord, he showed me that it
was not my *little writings* at all that
was wanted; but that His gracious
dealings with me, should be used as
a help to others. I saw it, and was
humbled.

I then gave my permission, and re-
quested the publisher to send me such
articles as he had chosen, so that I
might revise them. When they came
I felt no liberty to touch them. They
were each a simple statement of some
new experience born along the lines
of conflict; and upon the arena of life's
battlefield. So I returned them to him
as they were.

And I trust as these pages are pe-
rused, that the writer will be lost sight
of, and only the Divine tracery seen.

A. E. B.

CONTENTS.

"There's never a rose in all the world,
    But makes some green spray sweeter;
There's never a wind in all the sky,
    But makes some bird's wing fleeter;
There's never a star but brings to heaven
    Some silver radiance tender,
And never a rosy cloud but helps
    To crown the sunset splendor;
No robin but may thrill some heart,
    His down-like gladness voicing,
God gives us all some small sweet way,
    To set the world rejoicing."

INTRODUCTORY.

MEMORY stretches over a lapse of years since first I gave my young heart to God. The first sixteen of which, with its varied phases, I will pass lightly over. Suffice it to say, that sometimes I would tread the narrow way, then my feet would slip into some by-path which led me far from the cross of Christ.

The next seven years furnish a dark picture. The cruel monster, Death, entered my home, and in two years a kind husband and three lovely children were laid low by his merciless power. With idols smitten, hopes blasted, and heart crushed, I went forth from my once happy home *alone!*

How bitterly was that word engraven
in burning characters upon my soul!
How I writhed under those heavy
strokes, and rebelled against God.   I
fully appreciated poor Mrs. Job's feelings when she told her husband to
"curse God and die."

With too much pride to let people
know how much I suffered, I would
hide those dark depths of suffering
and rebellion beneath a smiling face;
yet my most intimate friends, knowing the facts in the case, in spite of
my high head and defiant mien, would
sometimes tender me their pity.   But
my proud heart, bleeding at every pore
would not accept anything which savored of sympathy.   On one occasion
one of my dearest friends, my pastor's
wife—said to me : "My husband and
myself sympathize deeply with you in
your sad bereavement.   We pity you

much." I replied: "I do not want your sympathy. I scorn it. I scorn pity from any source. If you have no sentiment but pity, don't offer me that, for I hold it in contempt." My looks and tones, inspired by the same fearful pride, confirmed my woe. She sweetly replied : "We have other than pity—we love you much." I said: "I will accept your love—your pity I scorn."

The yearning of my heart, like the tendrils of a vine, were continually reaching forth for something around which they might entwine themselves; for I had not yet learned that there was a fullness in the Gospel of Christ to satisfy every demand of the human soul. My heart and my flesh cried out, not for the living God, but for my dead idols. I literally worshipped at the shrine of the dead, spending hours among my graves, prostrating myself upon them, begging God to let me die. Life was such a burden it seemed I could endure it no longer.

But has not this dark picture any brighter shades, any relieving tints, any blue skies? Yes, there were occasional rifts in the clouds, from which gleamed some sweet promise of God; under its genial rays my pride, rebellion, and the clinging of my nature, would melt and yield sufficiently to bring me some consolation of the Gospel. Then I could endure for a little time the intensity of furnace fires. But soon they would begin to scorch, and again I would charge God with injustice and partiality. With my face to the floor, I would say: "Oh, God, thou has broken and cast down all that was dear to me, Thou hast smitten my idols, now smite me."

These terrible scenes lasted generally from one to two hours, when the tempest spent its fury, and I was calm again. I would then bathe my face, assume a smile, and go out into the world, none dreaming what a terrible tempest I had been through. But some of my keen-eyed friends would discern the fearful under-current, and kindly whisper: "The Lord loveth whom he chasteneth." I said : "Don't talk that to me, I do not believe it, if the Lord loved me he would never torture me like this."

I saw no reason why I should suffer thus. I prayed God to show me why he dealt thus bitterly with me. After a time He began to mirror to my view my real condition. Little by little He unveiled the interior of my heart and showed me myself. And O, what a spectacle! What depths of depravity ; what pride and rebellion. I had

oftentimes wondered : If I was a child
of God, why was my soul the thea-
tre of these many conflicts. When
I looked into the deeper strata of
my heart, I found the answer. I
saw, too, in the Book of God, a page
of Christian experience far in advance
of me, and how was I to attain it, was
the all absorbing question. I had
been instructed to "work out my own
salvation," so I set about it with bit
and bridle, to curb *this* element of my
nature, and control *that*. But the
first I knew some feeling of pride
would possess me, and with a haughty
toss of the head, I would give expres-
sion to it. Then I would go before
God humbly craving His pardon,
wondering why he did not keep me
when I so much desired it. I would
then go on nicely for a little time,
obeying God the best I knew how,

when suddenly I would be overtaken
with another of those terrible tempests
of rebellion and wounded idolatry;
and what I suffered in these, no human being ever knew.

Many times a day would my wretch-
ed heart breathe its longings to God
for deliverance, and for inward purity.
I hardly knew why I prayed thus, for
theoretically I did not believe in any
distinctive feature in Christian experience, denominated "purity or perfect
love." But however crooked my
theory, practically the needle was true
to the pole, and I was instinctively led
to the *Who* instead of the *what* for deliverance.

As I began to walk up to my light,
more dawned. I saw the whole thing
was summed up in two words : *consecration* and *faith*. Then came the
tug of war. For months I prayed,

day and night, that I might be enabled
to make a full surrender to God of all
my powers. Some things would go
on the altar, and some would not.
This struggle continued till Septem-
ber, 1867, when my whole being was
presented a living sacrifice to God.
The things I had clung to became
such a loathing to me, and I was so
hungry for God, that it seemed I could
not live without Him. Everything
went on the altar. In just a moment
the tempests fury swept past me and I
entered into rest, and O, such a rest!
how much it meant to me. My strug-
gles were all over and my conflict
ceased. When I arose from my knees
such a holy calm possessed me as I
never knew before.

Days and weeks passed, and still
that rest continued. I had no emotion
of joy, praise, or anything: it was just

a dead calm—a perfect rest, a sense of inward purity: my whole being seemed like a sheet of white paper, without a blot or stain upon it. My whole experience was summed up in two words: Rest and Purity. How grateful was that experience to my poor heart; just what I wanted—just what I needed.

Thus I went on until October 21st when my consecration received a severe test. The last item of my consecration, that which was the hardest to get on the altar—was the first to be tested. For two hours I was dumb before God, I could only look the matter over, and weigh it in my newly adjusted scales. How the matter would turn I knew not. But I saw no will of my own in the matter, simply suffering. At length I bowed before God, and said from my inmost soul: "O, my God, this consecration shall stand the test if I die in consequence of it." I think I did not say another word. I had no sooner breathed that out, than such an avalanche of God's glory came upon me as I had never dreamed of. I was completely submerged and overshadowed with the Divine Excellency, I arose from my knees, wondering what had come upon me. And all night I lay so hidden away in God, that I seemed to know nothing of earth.

Nearly all of the succeeding day I spent in my room alone with God and lost in His immensity. What a day that was to me! At night I retired early and slept like a babe in its mother's arms, which I had not done for seven years. How could I sleep during those wearisome days and nights? But the Rubicon was passed. I slept sweetly till the sun was up. When I

awoke the first thought was: "He giveth His beloved sleep." Every day I
was so overpowered by the Divine
glory, that I could only kneel in silent
adoration before God. I could not
ask for anything more, for I did not
want anything more. I often used to
say: "Stay thy hand, Father, I can
bear no more."

How I loved seclusion with God.
The presence of my best friends seemed
an intrusion. My Bible was my constant companion. Its sacred pages
would open up such hidden depths,
and unfold so fully the lovely character of my Divine Conqueror, that I was
lost in wonder, love, and praise. Like
a simple child (as I was), I would kiss
the sacred Volume, and say : "'Thy
word O God, is sweeter to me than
honey and the honey-comb." Had
any one asked me: "Do you ex-

pect ever to have any trials or temptations?" Such was my simplicity and ignorance that I should have answered: "No." I thought my whole future would be one eternal noonday of God's sunlight. Having been kept in the furnace till I was purged from all the dross of my nature, as I thought, where was the need of further trials? I had not yet learned that it takes just as intensely heated furnace to test the gold as it does to purge it. I thought I stood complete in Christ, not knowing that it would require years of storm and sunshine, heat and cold, adversity and prosperity, for my character to take on completeness and maturity, as the sequel has proved.

The long continued strain upon my nervous system, induced by bereavement and mental agony, had greatly impaired my health. But now I found

my health much improved under the
new regime. I was soon able to return
to the store, from which I had been ab-
sent nearly a year. But how could I
retain my newly found treasure and engage in business? My position in the
store was a responsibe one, and would
it not interfere with my abiding com-
munion? Would not my intercourse
with the public break this sweet spell
which was over me so continually? I
feared, not knowing the magnitude or
permanence of the work wrought in
me. I felt I would rather live in a
prison-cell on bread and water all the
rest of my life, with my indwelling
Savior, than to engage in anything
which would break his power over me.

The Lord showed me that if he
could save me so completely from indwelling foes, he could save me from
outside influence. I entered upon my

duties, and never did business so easily in my life. Everything seemed to go like a well regulated machine. My head and my hands did the execution without reaching my heart; as I walked to and from the store, the grass, the stones, and the side-walk, seemed to be all praising God. Indeed, my life was one complete doxology. The very circumstances which had made me so miserable, though still existing, were attuned to my new condition, and all blended in one harmonious strain.

This condition lasted many months before I knew anything of the crucifixions which have since come into my life, and as they began to manifest themselves, I have been shown the needs be for them, till I see nought but God's hand in it all.

FOOTPRINTS
OF A
PILGRIM,
IN THE
WHATSOEVER-WALK.

HIDDEN RECESSES.

THERE are hidden recesses in the divine life where only God and the individual soul commune; where we are so shut up in Him, that nothing can touch us except through Him, and so solitary and alone are these steppings we are conscious of being taught directly by Him.

As we thus walk, how marvellous are the Divine manifestations. That God should speak so directly to us, surpasses anything we had ever before experienced.

There are times when I am not permitted to read my Bible, to the end, that He, the blessed Holy Spirit, may take some of the words therein written, and bring them unto me in a more direct way. As the state of my soul indicates a need, then they are *truth*, then they are *life*, beyond anything known in the more formal reading.

I have been passing through strong testings for many months, until it seemed that the end must·be near, so great was the pressure. But it has been shown me lately, as never before, that we are often called to bear the states and conditions of others, that like the Master, we may be the better prepared to succor the suffering and sorrowing ones.

Humanly speaking, He could not succor or save to the uttermost on every point, except He first passed through the same. It became a necessity for Him to taste of every bitter cup, and bring Himself to our level, in order to lift us up from those same conditions.

Thus it behooved Him to suffer in the flesh, in all of the phases of interior crucifixion, passing through death upon all points, that we might be able to follow Him on those lines. To "follow the Lamb whithersoever He goeth," means more and more to us, as we advance in the regenerate life, and I am glad that it is *His* to lead, and *ours* to follow.

To follow Him through reproach, denial of friends, through betrayal, and through false accusation without offering a word of self-vindication or explanation, but to walk in continual consecration to the cross of Christ, is but a small part of *the following*. It means much of plucking out right eyes, and cutting off right hands. Not simply some unnatural protuberance, but something as dear to the heart, as the right hand to the body, and tender as the right eye.

In the days of John Wesley, there lived among the miners of England, a gross, ignorant, wicked fellow, whose only affinity was his large bull-dog, whose pugilistic tendencies paralleled those of his master. They were both a terror to the people. To the surprise of all, the Spirit of God got hold of the man, and he became thoroughly converted. He was appointed a leader over a class of Christian miners, and while he was being used very successfully in leading many to Christ, he was himself taking on growth and maturity, and of course was led through channels of crucifixion.

One day some person was passing through a forest, and saw him digging a grave. Waiting, unobserved, to watch results, he saw him embracing his dog very tenderly, and heard him say : "My dear, faithful friend, I have loved you long and much, but dear as you are to me, you must die by my own hand, for I cannot let you come between the Lord and my heart." After another affectionate embrace, the faithful creature died by the hand of his master, and was buried in the newly made grave. The self-sacrificing man went to his field of labor feeling that in plucking out the right eye he had removed the last substance which was likely to cast a shadow between God and himself.

Oh! God, bring me *there* at any cost. I know it is a solitary way. The multitudes do not throng there, nor are little companies grouped along its isolated path. The church does not walk there, nor do friends tread its narrow court, for it excludes earthly friendships, and every thing else that savors of the human.

And with each varying phase of crucifixion and death, comes the being taken farther, and still farther into the hidden recesses of the Divine, till, like the deeper symphonies of the sea, while the waves are dashing high and fierce above, fathoms below are divine harmonies and sweeter melodies than can ever be dreamed of from any other source. The rhythm and undulations of this music as they flow through the soul, quiet every power of the being, and only God is known.

> "In the heart of the sea
> There's a symphony sleeping :
> There is wafted to me
> From the heart of the sea
> A divine melody,

Mingled laughter and weeping ;
In the heart of the sea
There's a symphony sleeping."

THE TRANSPOSED SCALE.

THE primary lessons in singing are in the natural. In it, are em-bodied all the rudimentals of a future course. In it, the pupil makes his most uncertain sounds, in it, he makes his first proficiency; and in it, he bears away his first palm.

But as soon as he becomes sufficiently familiar with these first principles, the scale is transposed, another key is in-troduced, the music is written on a little higher key, perhaps. The voice adjusts itself to the new key, and the practice commences. When lo ! as he begins to think himself an adept in this key, another transposition occurs

—another key still is introduced, upon which all his music lessons are written. The "incidentals" are new, besides some "*accidentals*," perhaps, which may be a little humiliating to the pupil sometimes, nevertheless, they have their mission.

Again the scale is transposed ; still another key is introduced with its incidental sharps, flats, and rests. The pupil eager to touch every note, inadvertantly sings a "*rest*," when to his mortification he has produced discord; the teacher then brings him back, drilling him on the change of tone thus indicated, as well as the *no tone*. And so the transposing goes on, getting farther and farther from the natural, till all the seven helps are reached. As he advances the music becomes more complicated. The key changes very abruptly ; also the *time*.

Rests of various lengths are introduced, alternating with notes of sound.

When through a protracted course of discipline and practice he masters difficulties, becoming proficient in all of the transposed scales, so that he can render with ease any complex music, with any change of key, time, rhythm, or metre, he is even then perfected through practice: and as he still goes on his motto is: "Practice makes perfect."

And as in the *New Song*, there is a full counterpart of all the distinctive features in the lesson.

LOSING AND FINDING.

"He that findeth his life, shall lose it: and he that loseth his life for My sake, shall find it."

The above sacred words were given me very suddenly one day, some months ago: and with them came a beautiful hush of soul. I seemed ushered into the inner sanctuary of Divine life, and light, and love. Many days passed, and these words still floated through my soul like liquid music, with the rhythm and melody of a sweet song. I knew it meant much to me, but how much, was beyond my ken. I said many times during that Divine visitation, "I will lose my life, Father, on any point that Thou shewest me."

In about two weeks, I was brought to a sudden and painful test. God in his providences, showed me a point, upon which I was to yield up my life. It was a very vital point, and I knew not how much so, until called to give it up. Then came a conflict between the flesh and the spirit. The spirit in its obedience, said: "I will yield up my life, I will lose it for His sake." Yet the flesh clung, insisting that I should give an explanation of circumstances, and that would bring about an amicable adjustment of matters. But a diviner Voice whispered : "That would be seeking to save your life." I replied: "Yes, Lord, I will lose my life. I will yield it up." Still the tenacious clinging of my nature would not let go ; and for ten or twelve days, my soul was a theater of conflict, till one day the conflict suddenly ceased. As the smoke and din of battle cleared away, I found I had lost my life on the point in question, and a new life had taken its place. The old hush of soul returned, and a spirit of gladness possessed me. I was so glad of the Divine manifestation first given me to prepare me for the contest, and glad for the requisition made upon that life so dear to me. Glad also, that God so graciously held me to the test, till the work was finished. Weeks passed and that life came back to me, that which I had lost I found again. But Oh! so changed, I scarcely recognized it; so pruned off and shaped anew it seemed like another life, which it was. The mixture of the human seemed gone, and I held it for God.

Now I hold it for Him alone. Now, I know in a newer and a fuller sense, what it is to lose a life throbbing with the warmth of its vital forces, and find it again, thus proving how literally we may find what we lose for God. But so complete was the losing, that there was no desire for finding it, but wholly unsought, God graciously gave it back, sanctified and fit for the Master's use. And so all the way along, we can only know of the grand possibilities of the divine life, as we are pushed by the direst extremities.

TREADING THE WINE-PRESS.

A SHORT time ago, I dreamt I saw a strange looking structure of heavy timbers ; though most of it was underground, and could only be seen from one side, yet it loomed up very formidably and mysteriously.

A dear minister of the Gospel (who is now deceased), called my attention to the underground part of it. There I saw a large wine-vat out of which several persons were dipping the pure juice of the grape at wholesale rates, with buckets and pails of various sizes, for the benefit of others. Above it lay a heavy timber horizontally, down which was trickling in tiny streams the crimson fluid which was yielding such ample supplies for the many. I gazed in great admiration and wonder that such life currents should flow so freely with no visible pressure principle. Not understanding it I turned to go away, but under the power of its mysterious attraction, I turned back to gaze upon its strange workings. There I stood wondering where the heavy pressure so fraught with such grand results was, when I awakened with a profound impression upon me, of what, I hardly knew. Immediately a soft, sweet voice whispered " I have trodden the wine-press alone!" I recognized the voice and the fact; I said "Yes, Lord; and what about it? What would'st Thou teach me in reference to it?"

Soon He began to interpret it by showing me that Christ trod the wine-press alone, not only single-handed, but in secret silence. In his walks among men they saw his goodness and greatness, but they knew not the in-

terior process of crucifixion going on
all those years. They knew not that
all which pertained to His human was
subjected to a continuous crucifixion
(though He had never sinned). They
saw the outward manifestation but
knew not what it had cost, and was
costing him. They afterwards saw
him nailed to the cross in the exterior
act of crucifixion; then they knew it
was attended with great suffering.
But they knew not at what an expense,
and how continuously the life current
trickled from its warm fountain as it
flowed into the great ocean of salvation, whereby such myriads receive
Eternal Life.

" For none of the ransomed ever knew,
How deep were the waters crossed,
Nor how dark was the night which the Lord
  passed through,
Ere he found his sheep that was lost."

He also showed me, that they who are committed to "follow the Lamb whithersoever he goeth," are taken over the same line. Interior crucifixion of the natural, till naught of ambition, taste, affection, wish or preference lives. The body and its lawful appetites and desires is brought under till the whole is crucified, and lives only in God. In all of these they have died in the *natural*, but so quickened in the *spiritual* that not an element of their character becomes annihilated, but quickened into Divine life till they only live and walk in God. Whereas they once craved human sympathy they now suffer in silence and alone. And as the Gethsemane experience of the Master was a part of his crucifixion, and there largely *He trod the wine-press alone*, so our Gethsemane experiences enter into our crucifixion also. And as

He passed through the crooked Via
Doloroso (a street of sorrows), to the
place of outward crucifixion, so we
have to tread the same zig-zag way of
sorrows,some times headed *this* way,
and some times *that*, till we know no
points of compass save that it is *the
royal way to the cross.*

After having thus with Him trodden
the wine-press alone we are so emphat-
ically "not of this world," we are not
much sought after or enjoyed by others,
unless they be hungry souls, or suffering ones ; and they can never know
till they have passed through it, what
it has cost us to be able to succor them.
They know not to what an extent the
corn of wheat has fallen into the ground
and died that it may bring forth much
fruit.

"For we which live are alway de-
livered unto death for Jesus' sake, that

the life also of Jesus might be made manifest in our mortal flesh. So then death worketh in us but life in you."

THE "WHATSOEVER STATE."

PAUL learned in "whatsoever state" he was "therewith to be content." An important factor in the case was, that he had to learn the lesson while in the "whatsoever state" and not in advance of it. We can never learn a spiritual lesson *until we come to it* in our experience. In the "whatsoever state" of the thorn in the flesh, he accepted obediently what he saw was in the Divine plan; and when he had thus accepted, he was so content therewith, that he would not have it otherwise. The next step was the "taking pleasure" in it, for he saw that through it, the power of Christ rested upon him.

In the "whatsoever state" of "stripes above measure," of "prisons more frequent," of "deaths oft," of "the Jews' thirty-nine stripes, five times," of being "beaten with rods," of "being stoned," of "being shipwrecked," of "being weary," of "suffering pain, hunger, cold, etc., etc.," he learned in each separate state, or under each circumstance "therewith to be content." Had he rebelled against it, feeling that his lot was hard, it would have been a barrier to the real contentment which follows close after we accept in God, the "whatsoever state, "or circumstance.

We read the above list of Paul's sufferings, almost in a single breath, but it took him years to go through the different phases, or in speaking of it disconnectedly, as the most events occur in our human life, he was years passing through the "whatsoever states,"

and learned his lessons one by one as
they came due. "O," you say, "that
stretches over such a number of years,
I want to learn quicker, and be made
perfect sooner." Hold on, dear friend,
everything in the spiritual life as in
the natural, is subject to the laws of
growth and development, and everything comes in its own order and time.
Paul could not learn to be *content* with
prison life, in his "thorn in the flesh"
experience. Nor could he have learned
to be content with the "stripes above
measure," while he was simply "in labor more abundant." But in *each
state* he learned to be content, not only
in it, but *with* it.

In the variety of his states and circumstances, every point of his character was assailed, and on each point as
it was assailed, there was wrought out
that which brought him into closer

fellowship with Christ in his sufferings,
and a consciousness of such contentment, he would not ask to have it otherwise—glad to have it so—took pleasure in it. Had there been left one
point unassailed, there would have been
one point which the Holy Spirit could
not have used as a medium of communication to the many struggling souls
that should follow after.

In view of it all Paul said: "Be ye
followers of me, even as I also am of
Christ." Dear child of God, as you desire to be made perfect, be ye therefore
a follower of Christ, as was his servant
Paul, and in "whatsoever state" you
are, there and then, learn to be perfectly
content. No matter how you came
there, Paul did not place himself there,
but in following Christ he found himself in the exigencies which alone could
prove such a means of grace to him.

ONWARD STEPPINGS.

ALAS! for the abnormal conditions which give such poor spiritual appetites and weak digestion. Alas? for the large class of spiritual babes, hanging upon the breast of human consolation. I am certain we can never appropriate strong meat, until we become weaned; for the affilliative forces of our being can never develop, until they are called into action. Milk and pap make fat babies, and pretty ones, who are so winning and sweet in their manner as to bring admiration from every one. But such have no muscle, no maturity of understanding, and no power of endurance; for nothing has ever come into their dear little lives to open channels of strength.

God has been pleased to take me over some pretty rough stepping these months past, He has led me over new and strange ways. I suppose if we were always taken over the same lines of travel, we should only be exercised on those lines of interior life which are involved in our steppings, and that would do away with that symmetry of character which pertains to wholeness. I can see, that, had Christ the Lord, left one point of character untouched during His walk on earth, that point, would be more than a match for some of us. When He said: "I have overcome the world," Oh! He meant so much, that can never be understood, only as it becomes due in our steppings.

I was once walking the street in New London, Conn., near the harbor, where many vessels of different kinds were lying. I noticed one whose name was conspicuous for brilliancy. It read to me: MARY CARNOLD. I thought what a queer name. Mary Carnold, had anything but a harmonious sound to me. But I kept walking on, until I got close enough to see a punctuation mark, which made the name on the vessel read: MARY C. ARNOLD. That solved the problem, and made me to see, that a distant view could not possibly unfold the finer points which were very apparent when we got to them. How many fine points in our lives, are discernable only as we approach them, then, after we have learned them at a great cost, how dear they are to us.

When we have dwelt long under the shadows of the cross, nothing is half so sweet to us as that. No flowers, which bloom along the highways of life, yield such perfume, as those under the shades of the cross, so delicate, so inspiring.

SUFFERING WITH HIM.

WE are not only members of Christ's body, but members also of one another, and just in proportion as we live in Him who is our Head, are we one in fellowship and in suffering with one another. I see so much virtue now in suffering, that I rarely shrink from it these times.

Were not all the different ingredients of bitterness put into our cup, and it pressed to our lips, till we drink to its very dregs, how could we help others in those different phases? The Master (humanly speaking), could not do it, much less we ; and the closer our union with Him, the more it is given us to bear the states of others, or in other words, pass through the various states of suffering which different ones are called to experience, not only to the end that we may better appreciate the conditions of the many, but that we ourselves may have the most perfect symmetry wrought out in us. And that symmetry is not complete when we come into a state of acquiescence even; but to take pleasure in infirmities that the power of Christ may rest upon us, is brought about by continuous sorrow and suffering, after the passive acquiescence comes upon us.

A great sorrow had been on me for a long time; a soul sorrow. Perhaps, it was in part born of circumstances. Nevertheless, it seemed "my soul was exceedingly sorrowful, even unto death." I seemed to be living in the 53rd chapter of Isaiah, more than any other phase of the Christ-life.

Yet in all of my walk with God, I was not permitted to ask Him to lift it; but could only accept and *endure*, as did the Master, knowing that through this I was brought into diviner fellowship with Him in His sufferings.

One day, as I was bowed low under the heavy weight, a sweet little voice spoke to my soul these words: "Can ye drink of the cup that I drink of? and be baptized with the baptism that I am baptized with? I said: "Yes, Lord, with all its bitterness, if Thou wilt stand by and uphold me."

I happened to look into my mirror one day, and saw that my visage was marred by the great sorrow, more than ever before, and the form bowed under its weight, and immediately again the little undertone whispered: "His visage was so marred, and His form more than the sons of men." He showed me that nothing could so mar the visage and form, as soul sorrow; and I accepted it with all it meant to me.

So greatly was I affected physically under its pressure, that a heavy trip-hammer throbbing was continuously in my brain, down the spine and nerve centers, till the flesh was wearied with its pulsations.

But I was to endure it, and thereby fill up the measure of His sufferings left behind, until it seemed that all His incarnated life was outlined in my soul, and I bowed under its weight, but accepted it all.

Immediately following this, I retired under the usual pressure of soul, and after enduring the dreadful throbbing of nerves of which I spoke, till a late hour, I dropped to sleep, and during the night, the Lord spoke to me in these words: "In walking with Christ *to* God, we walk with Him *into* God." These words sounded strangely sweet to me, yet I did not waken till morning. I then found that something had gone out of my life, and something had come into it, which still abides. That dreadful throbbing was gone, and has never returned. Circumstances remained unchanged, yet nothing hurt me. The smiting of the smiter continued, but gave me no pain. The words of Professor Upham's immortal poem :

"Smite on, it doth not hurt me now,
The spear hath lost its edge of pain,"

were repeating themselves in my heart constantly. I was held in great soul hush. My feet seemed like hinds feet. The birds sang sweetly, and all nature joyous ; whereas before, all of nature's realm seemed a Gethsemane.

O! what power in those mystic words spoken to me that night ; and my life has been so changed since. Every remembrance of it, is like the melody of some far away song, as it floats through my life. It soothes and charms, as only the voice of God can.

BEAUTY ON THE ASH HEAP.

IN the Old Dispensation, when a young pigeon, or a turtle-dove was brought for a whole burnt offering the first thing done, was to pinch off its head ; the next, to take away its beauty. We are told, that in the East, the plumage of the turtle-dove is very beautiful ; blue, green and purple commingled with gold, making it such a thing of beauty, as to be held in great admiration.

But that feature of beauty has to be plucked off, and deposited where? On the altar? No ; but upon the heap of ashes, then carried outside the camp

where all refuse matter is deposited.
First, cast down within the temple,
then, borne without the camp! Then
the cleft body is subjected to the altar
fires, and it burns "all night unto the
morning."

So of the anti-typical. After having
arrived at that phase of progress in
the divine life, where the soul is called
to present itself as a whole burnt offering, the head has soon to come off.
The soul has to give up its theories
and preconceived opinions, its reasonings and questionings. Soon again it
is despoiled of any attractions it may
have, or *seem* to have.

The beautiful plumage, whatever it
may be, is plucked off, and instead of
being laid in a very orthodox way upon the altar, and subject to altar fires,
it is borne, even by human agencies
outside the camp, amid contumely and

reproach, and thrown upon the ash heap with all that is obnoxious and revolting to natural taste and refinement.

Then, the plain matter-of-fact offering, is laid upon the altar of the temple (which temple is the Lord God), and subjected to a slow, smouldering fire, in silence and in darkness all night unto the morning, when it is consumed.

Other worshippers are gratified with their brilliantly-lighted altar fires, so replete with divine manifestation and human admiration. They sing of "Beulah Land" with its blossom and song; and of the "Bliss of the Purified," etc., which is all good and sweet, and perfectly legitimate on that plane. But on the *beyond line*, the decapitated burnt offering, has not only cast down its human reasoning, which has in the past so exalted itself against the knowledge of God, but it finds itself in close fellowship with Christ, in that phase of his character spoken of by Isaiah, as being "without form and comliness, and no beauty that any should desire him."

That same soul had once been as greatly admired, perhaps, for its personal attractions as any had been. It may have had a wide influence in church or community, perhaps it possessed great brilliancy of mind, or of conversational powers, great wealth or social standing. But the beautiful plumage is gone! It is reduced to great simplicity. In prayer its words are few, its petitions *pre*scribed, and *pro*scribed by the Holy Spirit of God, for by this time the soul has become a worshipper in spirit and in truth, to an extent hitherto unknown to itself. In dress, in conversation and in gen-

eral deportment there is great simplicity manifest, so much so, that it is
regarded by others as being very
common-place, and is often shunned
by them. Not because they have not
confidence in its true character, but
because there is no beauty (according
to human conception), that any should
desire it. Its beauty is a thing of the
past, itself reduced to nothing but ashes, and all together are carried outside
the camp and there left amid reproach,
a gazing-stock for men and angels, con-
sidered as the filth and offscouring of
the world.

But is there really no beauty? Oh!
yes; for He giveth beauty for ashes,
and the oil of joy for mourning. Then
the King's daughter is all glorious
within. Then He saith: "Thou art
all fair my love, there is no spot in
thee." O blessed words! How they

distil heavenly dews upon the soul, till it drinks in the balmy air of Heaven to its blessed fill!

THE HOLOCAUST.

IN looking over my diary, I find something like this: "O my righteous God, how have I withheld from thee thy righteous due! When in my heart and spirit I would yield thee perfect homage, the flesh has revolted; sometimes it has involuntarily shrunk from fellowship with Christ in his sufferings. Pity and pardon me, O God, and help me now to bring my broken gift to the altar, and enter into a covenant with thee, by sacrifice of the whole being.

That was a long dark night to me. I felt its approach as the daylight receded little by little from my soul, till all was gone, and the darkness was so great that not a ray of light was reflected, not a star glimmered upon my pathway. I had walked by sight much of the time since the autumn of 1867, and even in much of my *faith*-walk, the star of hope, had beamed mildly through some rifted cloud, and I felt its anchor sure. But where was I now. The last territory I surveyed was surely Beulah land, to which its green pastures, and still waters, its birds of song, and flowers of beauty, would attest. The sunshine was almost perpetual, and if perchance it was shut in a little, the golden fringed cloud bespoke it shining still. True, many handfuls of wheat had been gleaned by the lowly Ruth. Upon many hearts, and over many altars was inscribed in letters of gold: "Holiness unto the Lord," through the weakest of instrumentalities, and that not without a spirit of labor and travail of soul. But that savored more of Gethsemane than of Calvary.

My case seemed almost a duplicate of that of Abraham's, who, when he asked God for a test of some matter, was told to bring a sacrifice whereby he should covenant with him. Abraham did so, and before the Lord practically regarded it, "Lo, an horror of great darkness fell upon him." Then, when it pleased the Lord, He explained the matter to him in detail. It was in the midst of Abraham's *faith and obedience*, that darkness closed its impenetrable portals around him, so that the whole matter was hidden from his consciousness. Abraham was tested in his obedience, and not in disobedience. And where am I? Had I disobeyed

God? Not consciously. I was obeying Him as far as I knew—walking up to my best light. But I was required to offer myself a *whole burnt-offering*, in a sense beyond anything I had ever understood before. Not a *sin-offering* —that had been offered and accepted previously. But, like Paul, after he had reckoned himself dead indeed unto sin ; after he could glory in the cross of Christ, whereby he was crucified unto the world, and the world unto him; self with its desires and preferences, innocent though they be, still existed, and sometimes their voices were heard above the still small voice of the Beloved. "Ah," you say, "these are so deeply implanted in our natures, that we can never get beyond them." But, beloved, give the reins into God's hands fully, and see if he does not take you beyond them. Consecrate your-

self to the cross of Christ, in a broader
and deeper sense, than you ever con-
ceived of before, and in due time you
will know something of what Paul
meant when he said: "I am crucified
with Christ." To see it written on the
sacred page presents the dim outline
of a picture which is only filled with
the practical details of a consecrated
life. To understand it is to know it
experimentally. Sometimes I would
give audience to reasonings and questionings, when simple faith was required. In stepping upon an untried
plank in God's platform, I found myself instantly philosophising and trying
it a little, before stepping out full
weight. I always feared fanaticism so
much, that when God called me to
travel some unfrequented path, rough
winding, and obscure; though it were
drawn in lines of sacred blood, I would

stop and look this way and that, to see if it were really of the Lord. If so, why were not the many in whom I had confidence as Christians, treading the same way? Always the answer came: "What is that to thee? Follow thou Me."

These are but instances of the many, which, though not formidable enough to offend, are subtle enough to ensnare. As I saw them, I cried heartily unto the Lord, that He would bring to the point of crucifixion, all the truant-forces of my being, that every strag-ling element might die the death. A burden of prayer came upon me, but so circumscribed in its form, that I could only pray continually: "Let Thy will be done in me perfectly." I de-sired the Divine Will to be perfected in me, more than I desired anything else. In a quiet hour these significant words interrogated themselves to me : "Are ye able to drink of the cup that I shall drink of, and to be baptized with the baptism I am baptized with ?" I said : "Yea, Lord, if thou wilt stand by me." After a little, I lost that spirit of prayer. When it became thoroughly lodged before heaven's throne, I lost sight of it, when lo, a terrible darkness enshrouded me completely, so dense and so strange ; unlike anything I ever had before. I seemed like one bewildered. I cried unto the Lord day after day, but all was silent. I reached out my hand for something whereby to locate myself, but could feel nothing. Again I cried : "Dear, Lord, what does this mean? Where am I? Have I grieved thee?" Still darkness and silence were the only responses.

I had forgotten that in the Jewish economy, the "whole burnt-offering" was a night sacrifice, "burning on the altar all night until morning." Nor was it laid upon the altar an undivided whole; the dissecting knife did its work first, severing a tie here, and piercing a joint there. Ah! the dissecting knife revealed the necessity of the altar fire. My flesh writhed, but my spirit said: "Keep me till my flesh yields to the death." It was not one circumstance alone, but several, and they seemingly disconnected, which God used for fuel to keep up the altar fires.

Weeks passed, and still no answer, except an occasional: "Be still, and know that I am God." Suffice it to say, when at last the day dawned, by its grey twilight I began to comprehend my situation, and with it I saw that the altar of sacrifice had done its work. The voices within were all hushed, save one whispering in an undertone:

"As God will,
And in His hottest fire hold still."

And I *did* hold still, for the Beloved was there.

As the flood of sunlight poured in upon the earth, I too, was bathing in the sea of gladness and brightness; for the glory of the Lord filled the temple. My place of sacrifice had become sacred to me. It had become my "trysting place with the Divine." As I walked out from the hallowed place, I hungered and thirsted for a more perfect knowledge of God. I said: "My God shew me thyself, in thine own way, whether by revelation, inspiration, or thy providences; only let me know more of thee." And so He does. Every day, the new unfoldings of His lovely character so eclipse everything else, as to shut me up with God, in a sense hitherto unknown. In every phase of my life, I see but the hand of God ; and I breathe the Divine Atmosphere continually. "The Lord is in his holy temple ; let all the earth keep silence before Him."

THE TWO SPONGES.

A FEW weeks ago, I prepared two sponges to grow small seeds for parlor ornaments. I filled the cells carefully with the seeds, put each sponge in a dish of water, and set them away in a cool dark place to germinate. At the expiration of three days and nights, I brought them forth ; and one sponge, which was a nice little pyramid of itself, had germinated most of its seeds. But one kind, though much swollen, had not quite burst their shells; so that sponge had to go back to its hiding place for another twenty-four hours.

Sponge No. 2, had sprouted but few of its seeds, and its general appearance was so unpromising, the poor thing had to be consigned again to darkness for several days. Watching its progress daily, my compassion was excited in its behalf, as I saw its tender blades reaching out so beseechingly for warmth and light, which I would gladly have given them, but too much was pending, even to satisfy an inherent law of their being. Other seeds of importance were in process of germination, and needed a dark, low temperature, to bring it about; though I feared it might be at the expense of those which had already taken on growth.

I was at length rewarded by seeing its little thread-like fibers covering the sponge: yet its different states of growth and development were so varied as to render it too disproportionate for beauty.

Sponge No. 1, was, meantime, taking on such symmetry, that its pyramid of verdure gave me great delight. But, alas! for its short-lived beauty; too soon its glory diminished; its little cells were too closely packed to allow expansion of root. Hence its foliage faded, and to-day I had to clip its yellow tops.

But how with sponge No. 2? Its formation was not favorable to early developments, hence its frequent seasons of darkness. But after its condition had become adjusted thereto, its capacity for growth and maturity was far greater than the other. And soon

its angular points, and disproportionate growths were superceded by sym-
metrical, proportionate and luxuriant
growth, till my minature garden became one lovely tuft of green.

While caring tenderly for them
both, I was deeply impressed with the
fact of two distinct classes of God's
people. The one class, for some reason understood in the great legislature
of the Infinite, is not enshrouded in
darkness so often, or so long ; yet they
take on growth, which gives them
symmetry, in the general sense ; and
are looked upon as the excellent of
the earth ; and used for various kinds
of vineyard labor ; but are not chosen
for out-post service.

Those of the other class, like Abraham, even while walking in obedience,
lo ! an horror of great darkness casts
its impenetrable folds around them,

till not a glimmer of light is seen. Those graces which have taken on growth, so earnestly long for a more congenial atmosphere, but it is denied them, till a purpose is effected. Some important seeds of divine truth have been, perhaps unconsciously, disseminated in precious soil; seed which cannot quicken into life, except it die; and that dying involves so much. But, after it becomes a living principle, and strikes the roots, deep in the Infinite, its branches take on divine foliage, and so hide angular points, that God sees greater conformity to the Model, the Image of His Son, than ever before; and they have borne much fruit to the glory of God. Then they understand the Divine declaration, "I will lead her into solitude, and there will I speak to her heart."

MORTIFYING THE FLESH.

"BUT if ye through the Spirit do mortify the deeds of the body, ye shall live," or in other words, if ye by following the Spirit, are led into phases which are mortifying to the flesh, by letting that mortification work death to the flesh, ye shall live the new or regenerate life. And this means to the follower of Christ on every plane of that following, all that he can possibly apprehend. It is consecutive in its openings to our conceptions, and is manifest to us only as we measure up to the standard of the manifestation.

For instance, we may walk in the humble consciousness of implicit obedience, so far as we know, and close union with God to-day, while to-morrow or next week, something may come into our lives which will bring

to the surface that which we did not
know existed. It has not yet become
sin to us, for the blood of Jesus Christ
has, we trust, cleansed us from all sin.
But some element of the being, *ingrain*
and *interwoven* with the very tissues
of life, that, without our consent, as-
serts itself as soon as it is hurt. Now
comes the test; shall we allow that
wounded element to assert its right,
and vindicate itself? On the natural
plane your sense of justice would say
"yes, and I'll resent it too." But,
if we follow Christ we subject it to
constant mortification, with all its pain
(and who ever knew a painless mortification?) till the conflict ends in death.
It may be a longer or shorter time in
dying, as the case may be, but is not
likely to die a practical death till first
brought to the surface. It often cul-
minates with a single act of the soul

at last, and sometimes that almost, or quite an involuntary act.

We may be precipitously plunged into the valley of humiliation ; its steep and rugged declivities may tear and hurt so painfully that it seems we can never rise again. But that tearing and hurting is only the mortifying of some "deed of the body," or element of the flesh-life ; and we are never to rise again on the side upon which we went down. We grope our way around its damps, chilled and smarting in our wounded parts. We writhe and struggle, trying to pray through it. But alas! it is not the kind through which we can pray, though praying greatly helps us, mortification has set in which must end in death. A corn of wheat has fallen into the ground, abruptly and without our consent, it must now die *with* our consent.

But, as these tissues of life are both *voluntary* and *involuntary*, after the voluntary forces have yielded up their life we must wait patiently, holding the mortified parts to the test till, perhaps, in a most unthought of moment the involuntary has wheeled into line, and the work is done! Immediately there opens up to us the most grateful haven of rest, which we did not dream could exist in such a rough and rugged place. We are so hidden in the pavilion of God that we could forever stay in its chambers of quietness and security, enjoying the luxury of its downy pillows; and he permits it for a time, when lo! almost unconsciously to ourselves, we are taken out of those stony depths, which we have learned to love so much. And, as we rise in the life of God we have left behind that phase of the flesh life, or "deeds of the body" which we *morti-fied* and *crucified*. But now we *live*, yet not we, but Christ liveth in us, in a broader and deeper sense than before ; and we walk in a greater "newness of life" than we could possibly have done but for the painful experience of mortification and death.

LIFE OUT OF DEATH.

WE start out in our earlier steppings in groups ; all along the line are companies with whom we exchange fraternal greetings, and they give us much joy and encouragement, In due time, as we follow on, our companions are reduced to "Peter, James, and John." But alas! in the fulness of time they also fail us. We take them along with us into Gethsemane, for we so crave human sympathy as we grapple with some element of the self-life, which we once thought innocent and legitimate. But "Peter, James, and John" fall asleep, while we are struggling and sorrowing, and we are left to die alone! for even the Father seems to withdraw Himself from us, and this needs be, else how could we die? for death could not do its work in the presence of the Life-giver. But the Life-giver can enter the chamber of death, where lie the pulseless elements of some vital point of our being, which has been engaged in the last conflict of its life, for it loved not its life, even unto death.

It got into the fire not by taking itself there, but by following the Christ, it found itself there; and it dare not recoil, hence it was numbered with "the third part which was brought through the fire."

Then follows the quickening as the Life-giver enters the place of silence! And now we walk forth in "newness of life," that new life which was born of death—that regeneration in which the Saviour says if we follow Him, we shall occupy positions of honor in the coming age.

We formerly spoke of the converted man as the regenerate man, which he is in its incipiency. But the long and slow developing process has revealed stages in the work of regeneration never dreamed of then.

THE CURRENTS, AND COUNTER-CURRENTS OF LIFE.

THE Greeks, also the Hebrews, indeed, all of the Orientals were accustomed to calling all that was vast, and to them boundless, the sea.

And we know the sea, or ocean has its currents and its counter-currents, which we sometimes call under-tow, meaning an unseen power which carries back into the ocean, that which is brought to the surface.

Sometimes it comes in on the crest of the waves very triumphantly; sometimes it comes seething and boiling with the angry billows, mixed with mire and dirt, which is either deposited in an unsightly heap upon the shore, or is taken by the counter-current back into the ocean.

A friend of the writer was once bathing in the ocean, when a strong under-current took her out beyond her depth. She felt herself going and resisted to the extent of her ability, till she found further resistance useless: she then gave herself up for the Lord to let her go under, or manage the case as He saw fit. Just then a propitious wave took her shoreward. But not until she had gone through the blessed experience of yielding up her life in the most literal sense. God saw that her work was not finished as the events of subsequent years have proved, for she has been greatly used for others, and is at the present writing carrying on a great work for God.

There is in us a strong proclivity to resist the counter-currents, till we become wearied with our resistance, not always knowing that the very things we resist, are those which God designs to take us out into His great depths.

And those refluent tides as they surge back into God are laden-ed with human ambitions, blighted hopes, and broken idols, to which we have clung with all the tenacity of our being. We have said we cannot give them up, but an unseen force has overpowered us, and we have gone under till the currents and counter-currents have so blended in God, that we could not tell one from the other.

There came an under-current into the life of a beautiful girl, when her father told the Lord on his return from victory, that whatever came forth from the doors of his house to meet him, should surely be the Lord's, and should be offered up for a burnt offering. What was the father's horror when he was met by his only child, his beautiful daughter. Painful as it was to them both, she accepted the situation with all of the fidelity of woman's heart, and said: "Let me alone for two months that I may go up and down the mountains and bewail my virginity," or in other words, let me go and bid my companions good-bye, those with whom I have passed my childhood days, those with whom I have played, my school-mates, my dear girl friends, for I am now going into solitude, I am now go-ing to minister in the tabernacle all the days of my life. While my mates will become mothers in Israel, I shall per-petuate my virginity within the pre-cincts of the tabernacle, and my father's family will cease with me. And per-haps her sweet young heart had another friend who was dearer to her than all of her girl friends ; and *that one*, had to be given up, for the plan of God had been outlined in the great Council Chambers of the Infinite, and must be carried out.

God designed that beautiful girl to spend her life in the hallowed calling of a vestal virgin in His holy taberna-cle, and everthing had to be sacrificed for it.

He took His own way to bring her into the valley of silence, where the perfume of censers from the altar of incense (like the ottar of roses) permeated the inner court, dissolving the odors of sacrifice from the outer court.

"And I have seen *thoughts* in the valley,
Ah, me! how my spirit was stirred!
And they wear holy veils on their faces,
Their footsteps can scarcely be heard,
They pass through the valley like virgins
Too pure for the touch of a word."

The grand noble girl did as she desired, then passed into seclusion forever. But the daughters of Israel spent four days with her every year, and that was more than she expected when she went into seclusion.

We sometimes hear Jepthah's vow called a "rash" one, but looking at the fact that the "Spirit of the Lord" came upon him, and, under the inspiration of that Spirit, he made his vow, we can only see that God wanted the lovely maiden to do His work; and He brought it about in His own way.

See the counter-currents as they surged into the life of the Master, from the wilderness to the cross. In Gethsemane when three times He prayed : "If it be possible," but God was silent to him, till in His great agony the blood stood upon His surface, and He had reached the limit of His human possibilities, when an angel was sent, not to comfort, but to *strengthen* Him for more suffering, after which came the greatest soul travail ever known, a soul travail without which the plan of redemption would have been incomplete. A soul travail known to many of His saints since to an extent which takes away sleep, appetite, and all, till it passes off, which it does not do, till it has done its work in the plan of God.

To speak of the refluent tides in the life of Paul, Madame Guyon, Fenelon, and a host of others, would elaborate this article too much. But it is sufficient to know that they were exceedingly turbulent, but they so took them into the great heart of God as to blend into divinest symphonies, which echo all down through the ages, in deeper and sweeter harmonies, for having passed through the discordant strain of the counter-currents of life.

WALKING WITH GOD.

THE desires of a soul on a stretch for God, ofttimes outrun its capacity for taking on the Divine Nature. Its yearnings for the perfect are so intense, it would fain get *there*, by leaps and bounds. But the slower process of walking is ordained. "Walk before Me, and be thou perfect," was spoken to Abraham; and that life of walking, lay along the path of sacrifice and obe-dience, involving much that was dear to him.

Could we like the hind, climb to higher altitudes by graceful leaps, or like the bird of passage, fly across the desert, and over the waste of waters to our place of destination, we should lose all the revenues accruing from the deprivation, toil and weariness of the dusty highway of life, or battling with the treacherous waves of the sea, which threaten to engulph, as they lash in fury about us.

Our capacity in the spiritual, as in the natural, only takes on expansion under pressure.

God brings to the surface, one thing at a time, and that has to be disposed of, before another is taken up. We could no more go through crucifixion on all points at once, than could our Master, whose long, slow process of interior crucifixion, was so hidden from human view, that no one knew what was going on. But when the last great act of exterior crucifixion took place, they stood aghast.

So with his followers, they are not understood while passing through the hidden process of death, but when it becomes apparent that the work of regeneration has been wrought, many exclaim, "I want such an experience." But while the point reached is what they desire, they are not willing to walk the rugged path leading to *it*.

"BEAUTY FOR ASHES."

M RS. F. D. Gage once spoke before the Floral Society at Vineland, and on the occasion exhibited a beautiful flower which she said grew from a heap of ashes. A few years before, her son was engineering a portion of Southern territory. Going through the malarious district so many of his men were sick that he thought it best to burn over the swamps, woods, &c. He did so, and the result was six months of continual burning and smouldering, slowly, but surely, till apparently the life principle was eradicated from soil and sub-soil. But after two years of desolation and sterility, a little plant appeared, developing in time a flower so rich in its loveliness, so rare in its beauty, as to fill the beholder with admiration and almost adoration.

It was submitted to floral experts for classification, which proved a problem they were unable to solve. They knew of no class to which it belonged, nor had they ever seen anything so beautiful, so they were obliged to let it stand alone in its beauty.

So in God's spiritual economy, what may be patent to mortal eyes is rich foliage, lovely mosses, lichens, &c., but underneath and all around is unseen malaria, and God, the great Engineer, sets in motion a train of circumstances, which adds fuel to fire, till all power of life seems to be extinct. Nothing but a heap of ashes is left, and that outside the camp, mixed with reproach and calumny, instead of occupying a respected position on the Altar in the Temple. Even the devout worshippers cast a look of commisseration upon the poor outcast, as in Paul's day, when he was regarded as the filth and off-scouring of the world. That phase exists till all promise of anything but death and desolation, becomes but a spectral relict of the past! The soul thus exercised does not sing: "What peaceful hours I once enjoyed," for an unseen Hand is laid upon it, and it accepts the present, not in *exchange* for the past beauties and glories, as some suppose, but in advance of them.

Then in the right time, there is wrought out the conditions favorable to the germination of great truth-seeds, so hidden that none suspected their existence; and in process of unfolding, there appear rare specimens of "*Beauty for Ashes*," which the wise of earth fail to classify. It is beyond their apprehension, they cannot trace the origin nor discern the character. And so, as we go through the various processes of evolution, we cannot always understand the unfoldings in ourselves, or one another; hence our inability to judge another's experiences.

PERFECTING OF THE SAINTS.

WHILE the tendency of the present age is to superficiality, yet there are many hungry ones amongst the flock of God, but alas! so few qualified to feed them. I was much interested and profited by a testimony I once heard given by a Methodist minister. It was this: During his term of preparation for the work of the ministry, in his early manhood, he was in the habit of holding meetings in the rural districts, walking long distances to preach. One Sunday as he was walking along, on his way to fill an appointment, the Lord met him on the

way, and in a very unmistakable and
impressive manner interrogated him as
to the intent of his life work, to which
he replied: "Why, Lord that I may
bring sinners to Thee." But the Lord
said: "How about My Sheep?" He
made answer: "I dont know, Lord;
I am not qualified to feed them, as I
am not in advance of them, but as
Thou hast wrought a work in me,
which has not been done in the uncon-
verted, *I can help them.*" But the
Lord showed him that his mission was
not accomplished in simply bringing
sinners to Christ; an important feature
in the work was the feeding of the flock
of God, and that he must become qualified for that. Just then new light
dawned upon him, which greatly dis-
quieted him, and he wished the Lord
had let him go on as he was doing before. Soon, however, his disquietude

amounted to a distress unbearable,
for God had lifted the veil, and shown
him himself as he had never seen
before ; but he thought he must go on
and fill his appointment at any rate,
but he did not go far, his conflict became so distressing. Seeing a barn in
the near distance, he went in, and
shutting the door, went into a manger,
and there and then gave himself to the
Lord, in a sense, of which he had no
conception when he started out. And
as he did so the glory of the Lord so
shone around that it dazzled him.
He did not know how long he had been
there, but thinking of his appointment,
started to go out, but such a holy be-
wilderment was upon him, that he
could not find the way out, and had to
go back to his trysting place with the
Divine, and remained so enrapt in God
as to take no note of time.

At last he arose again to go, and found his way out this time, and borne as it were on wings he found himself. at his place of meeting, where the congregation had been in waiting more than an hour. As he entered he simply raised his hands and said: "All hail!" when the people fell like dead men all over the house, and others were crying for mercy, so he had no preaching, but spent the whole time in praying with souls and seeing them set at liberty in God.

A great revival broke out from that time and place, sweeping over all that section of country.

Then with great meekness of spirit he remarked, "that all the success which had followed his labors was traceable under God to the work then wrought in him, and had taken on its developments since."

The minister has since ceased his labors, but his works *do* follow him, for he being dead yet speaketh.

I have many times recalled the beautiful and impressive manner in which he related the occurrence, and have felt the specific qualifications needed for the specific work to which we are called.

If it is simply to bring souls into conversion or sanctification, the preparatory work must precede it. But if to take others on through crucifixions and deaths, into the risen life in Christ, thus enabling them to walk in greater "newness of life," than could possibly be attained short of those "deaths oft," then certainly the qualifications and education has to come to us through inwrought experiences of our own, and God, who has made demand and supply such a perfect adjustment, brings to those whom He has thus educated, plenty of work to do on that line.

In these days spoken of by the prophet Daniel, when "many shall be purified made white, and tried," there are so many of the Lord's chosen ones, who are thus purified and made white, walking with Him in a very close relationship, who never expect the programme will be changed, and so when the testing comes they do not know what it means, and think they have surely gotten away from the Lord, and soon begin to cast away their confidence, and suffer great loss thereby.

Others, again, who have stood clear in their experience of sanctification and have been teachers and leaders on that line, God in trying to take them up on a higher plane, has to take them through scenes so new and strange that

they get confused and bewildered,
thinking that they have inadvertently
stepped over on the enemy's ground,
and he tantalizes and worries them
until they can in no wise define their
position, then God in some way puts
them in communication with some one
of His who has traveled over the same
road and canvassed the same territory,
and trodden it till weary and footsore.
There are so many we meet who have
not only surmounted obstacles most
formidable in their own lives, but who
have been very helpful to others; when,
lo! they are suddenly brought to a
standstill themselves, and in trying to
take observations, sun, moon and stars
have disappeared from the spiritual
horizon, and they are trying to push
through with all the fidelity and cour-
age imaginable, but it is all "dead
reckoning," with them, and they, too,

forgetting that the slow process of *walking* follows the faster one of *running* and *mounting up*, are wondering what it all means, and where it will end. But God sometimes takes a very little thing to tide them over the sand-bar where they have stuck so fast. Yet, I notice He never lets the little thing come until the right time arrives. The sand-bar has done its work, and all that has entered into the seeming uncertainties of their state and standing had their mission, and when God sees that the testings have measured up to the necessities of the case, He says: "It is enough," and the prisoner of the Lord goes forth on joyful wing, like the moulted eagle, with renewed strength, and so on to the end.

CONCERNING TEMPTATION.

IN answer to the query: "Do we ever get beyond temptation in this life?" I would say, that what cleansing *fails* to do, crucifixion *may* do.

While we are walking in the cleansing, we are dead to sin and sinful self, but death to the flesh—the sanctified flesh—is quite another thing. So long as there is life there is susceptibility of appeal to that life. These appeals are, what we understand to be temptations. They may be appeals to the highest and purest elements of our being, but if it be not in harmony with the plan of God for *that* element to respond, one of two things is inevitable, either a conflict must follow every time, or the soul must "yield up its life unto death," even the death of the Cross. If the latter, there is never again, any response to temptation on that point. It cost such a soul much to get there, many conflicts and victories followed, perhaps, for years. But there came a time, when that particular element, whatever it was, had to die. It was some right eye, hand, or foot, but what-ever it was, it was dear as life, and, when it came to the final throes of the death struggle, it seemed as though that soul was forsaken of God, and man, and in its anguish it cried out: "My God, my God, why hast Thou forsaken me!" For this kind of death, can never ensue, in the conscious Presence of the Life-Giver, so he retires, leaving the soul to die alone, so far as the con-sciousness of His Presence goes. Usu-ally this death is followed, shortly, by the being "risen with Christ," in a sense far beyond anything ever known before, and on that point, that soul walks in "newness of life" fully, with no mixture of the oldness of life; consequently, upon that point, there can never again be a susceptibility to temptation, though there still may be upon many other points.

I do not think that Christ our Lord ever went through temptation but once on the same point, for on each point He yielded up His life. When He reached Gethsemane, that was the hardest and last, till He reached the crowning act upon the Cross. His whole life was one of interior crucifixion. And when the last phase of death, that of exterior crucifixion took place, the people stood aghast! little dreaming that His whole life had been one of interior crucifixion.

I do not say that these cases are frequent in His followers. Alas! for the rarity, and probably, few ever reached that perfection, where, on the various points of their nature, they are beyond temptation.

True, it is a long, slow process, and the Master was thirty years, and more, going through it ; for it only ended in the tragic scene of the cross.

We generally go through but one point of crucifixion at a time. So with the many points of character we have, God has to take us over the various lines of travel, to bring into requisition the particular traits he wishes us to become crucified upon.

I doubt not the Spirit might save us from these points if He so willed, but in that case, we could never understand or appreciate the work wrought.

We must know what we are to be saved from in order to glorify Him, and it can only be done as it enters the arena of conflict.

This is a vital subject, and at *very great cost* have I learned the little I know about it. But I do know there are depths of the saving power of the Gospel never yet reached by the line and plummet of finiteness.

FRUIT BEARING.

WE can only give to others, that which has been incorporated into our own being, only instruct others as we ourselves are taught of God. How little we know of real soul-travail only as the power emanates from the Vine to the branch. And how unfitted we are to affiliate with the spirit of the age, after a few seasons of that soul-travail which is so deep that it seals all power of utterance, so that no word or petition can escape, except in that un-formulated manner which seems more like incense arising, than something more tangible. But it touches God and brings blessing to ourselves, as well as to those for whom we travailed.

WITHOUT WISH OR PREFERENCE.

THE prayer of Jesus (Luke xxii: 39 —44), that the cup might pass from Him, showed, that up to that time, He had a little preference, although it was so deeply imbedded in an underlying strata of His being, He was unconscious of it until that hour. But, no sooner did it come to the surface than it had to die under the pressure of obedience to His Father. He was then perfected and no farther need of His suffering in order to be "made perfect," but just in a condition to go through the greatest soul-travail the world ever knew.

An angel was sent, not to comfort Him, as many suppose, but to strengthen Him for suffering from which He no longer shrank, for He had ceased to suffer in the flesh-life in the sense of

having to suffer in order to be perfected. So, just in proportion as we have
ceased to suffer in the flesh where we
have been called to yield up our life, are
we qualified to travail in soul for others.
In passing through death in any phase
of the flesh-life we need not to be
specially strengthened for suffering,
for the effort to relax our tenacious
clingings to life cause the suffering.
And, instead of being strengthened,
we need to be weakened, as dissolving
nature has to be before it can die. But,
after death ensues, we are strengthened to suffer birth-pangs to the end
that others may be saved. And our
real soul-travail is measured by our
flesh-death.

Christ the Lord yearned after the
lost race and wept over Jerusalem with
tenderest love and sorrow, but no soul-
travail ever equalled that of Geth-

semane, because He was never so fully perfected before.

"And being made perfect He became the Author of eternal salvation unto all that obey Him." Had He been made perfect only in part He could have saved us only so far as He had gone. But He, having been perfected up to the last point of preference, even, is able to save us as far as He went Himself. And if we "follow the Lamb withersoever He goeth" we shall know of that "uttermost" salvation which takes us beyond any wish or preference, however innocent or legitimate it may be.

RIGHTLY DIVIDING THE WORD.

IN order to rightly divide the Word of the Lord, each phase of truth has to be apportioned to its belonging.

Divine truth is a vast whole, but has many parts and phases, and is capable of being viewed from different standpoints as it becomes due in its revolutions. All lines of truth are dispensational, and when rightly divided are harmonious, but when wrongly, much incongruity and confusion follows.

To apply the Levitical law to the antedeluvians, Christ's sermon on the mount to those to whom the Law was really given, or, the preparing of the ark against a watery deluge, to this age, would bring the direst confusion. And yet each were phases of truth divinely apportioned to the age in which they were due. Each harmonious and complete in itself.

Our Lord's commission to His chosen ones to preach the Gospel, heal the sick, raise the dead, cast out devils, etc., seems to have got strangely mixed

in the minds of many people and thereby so clouded their vision as to pre-
vent their seeing God's real truth.
Some say healing the sick and raising
the dead went hand in hand in the
Apostle's days, and when one becomes
obsolete the other does also. That the
power of raising the dead is no longer
in the Church, hence healing the sick
and casting out devils have ceased also,
and they reject the whole.

Others say, they are parallel lines of
truth, and having proved the healing
of the sick to be not only extant in the
Church, but a grand and rapidly developing truth which is belting the
globe with its power; they cannot
divorce it from the other (the raising
from the dead), so they try hard to get
up the faith to call their dead back to
life again. They pray with strong crying and tears, command in the name of

the Lord Jesus Christ, that death loose his icy grasp and let the captive go free. Then they wait and watch for the seal to break, the rigid eyes to unclose, and the breast to heave with inspirations of life. But alas! no such results are obtained, and disappointed and saddened, they go away to ask, why?

Let *us* ask, why? In Matt. x: 1—8, we read that Jesus called unto Him His twelve disciples and commissioned them: to preach the kingdom of heaven is at hand, to heal the sick, cleanse the lepers, raise the dead, cast out devils. And to whom were they to go? "Not into the way of the Gentiles, nor into any city of the Samaritans. But go rather to the lost sheep of the house of Israel."

In Matt. xi: 5. we see a fulfilment of that mission, as was the fact all through the Apostolic age.

In Luke x. the Lord "appoints other seventy." They were to "go into every city and place whither He, Himself would come." What was their mission? To preach the kingdom of God, heal the sick, and receive power to tread on scorpions, etc. But nothing about raising the dead.

Again, after His resurrection, He extended the mission of the eleven, viz:—to go into all the world, and preach the Gospel to every creature, to cast out devils, speak with tongues, and heal the sick. Not a word about raising the dead.

Now what may we infer from this? Methinks simply this, that which was given to the twelve, who were the representatives of the New Testament priesthood, and for the house of Israel, expired with the Apostolic age, excepting what was ratified to them when their mission was extended after His resurrection and that, blended with the commission of the seventy is perpetrated down through all ages of the Church, and harmonizeth perfectly with itself. But raising the dead was no part of that extended mission.

Now and then traditionary or legendary breezes waft to us a report that some time and somewhere a case of being raised from the dead has occurred. But investigation has proven it a myth and the best historical scholars of the age say that no real case, has occurred, since the Apostolic age.

BLESSINGS OF DARKNESS.

THE richest experiences ever dispensed to the soul, are those very obscure things which cast nothing but a shadow over human wisdom and reason. What lowliness of mind, yea, what perfect abnegation, it hath wrought in the profoundest depths of the soul. We have for weeks been passing through some of these labyrinths.

For a time we could see neither sky nor shore; and we knew something of the fight of faith, before we were through with it. O how blessed to trust God in the dark—and so dark! But the darkness of night brings out glorious constellations, which at first seem but a milky way; but gazing steadily through the telescope of God's Word, what definiteness and what magnitude they assume to us.

The astronomy of God's redemptive plan, is far more grand and glorious, if I dare to say so much, than that of his creative economy, sublime as I apprehend that to be. In the natural world if it were always sunshine earth would lose much of its beauty ; its verdant fields would be sere and yellow. Our lovliest flowers bloom in the darkness of night.

So God often brings his people into darkness when he wants to speak to them. You remember he required a sacrifice of Abraham, and while he was yet enshrouded in the great darknesss which had closed into impenetrable folds around him, God spoke to him, telling him that his seed should be ''a stranger in a land that was not theirs, and they shall serve them; and they shall afflict them four hundred years.''

Then, after giving him the details of the matter more fully, God showed his acceptance of the sacrifice, and not before. And when the four hundred years were up, Moses thought to deliver them; he made a mistake to begin with, and had to be taken down into Midian for forty years before he could get where God could use him.

Ah! those *Midian*-experiences, what a power for good they are to us. Like Moses we are taken down from our loftiness in the silence of *Midian-life* and, like Moses too, when God gets ready to use us, we are called out. We are often premature in our attempts to fill the plan of God. He sometimes outlines to us our work, and without waiting for him to give the signal we start out, only to see that we have made a mistake, and then we are consigned to the land of *Midian* and in its silence and darkness, learn our own ignorance and inefficiency. Like Moses we come out of it humbled and shorn of our self-sufficiency.

In the Highlands of Scotland is a

gorge, a deep, dark gorge, so deep and
narrow that no human foot ever trod
upon its slimy bottom, and only the
hiss of the serpent was heard. But
up its craggy sides were blooming,
beautiful flowers, far more beautiful
and fragrant than anything flowering
in the sunlight.

Travelers often beheld them with
great admiration, but could devise no
plan whereby they could be obtained,
till one day some English gentlemen
saw them, and were intent upon
procuring them, but knew of no way
of so doing, till they saw in the distance a shepherd's hut, whither they
wended their steps. Upon arriving
they saw a little boy who, upon being
asked if he knew of any means whereby they could be obtained, replied:
"nae, mon, I dinna ken." Whereup-
on they asked if he would allow them

to put a rope around his body and let him down to their level that they might procure them.

The little fellow knowing well the danger of such an exploit, refused. They offered him large sums of money; he looked at the money thinking of the help it would prove to his father. They watched his conflicting emotions as they played upon the child's face, when, after a time, he said, I will if you will let my father hold the rope.

But they said we are as strong as your father, we will let you down and bring you up as safely as your father. But, said the little fellow: "my father loves me." That was an argument they could not gainsay, so the father was called and after adjusting the rope the father let him · tenderly down as only a father can do. After procuring the flowers the child was drawn up with his little hands full of the beautiful flowers, which were given to the gentlemen and he received his reward according to promise.

And so we are often precipitously thrown into the valley of humiliation, into the deep and dark chasm, and coming in contact with its craggy sides, the heart is rent and the spirit wounded. But Father holds the rope and he looks with pitying eyes while we are struggling with elements of our nature for which we are not responsible ; characteristics which came with our birth, and which have attended all of our steps through life.

But he sees a necessity for our yielding up our life on the particular point indicated, and we must be held there till this is accomplished. We writhe about and pray for deliverance, but it is all so dark and silent. We sometimes hear the hiss of the serpent and are frightened, but we are kept there, till God's plan is accomplished in us. And so we struggle on, and suffer on, till we reach the supreme moment of our life, then almost without any conscious act of the soul, the struggle ceases and we are at rest, and such rest, none can ever know who have not passed through a similar experience.

Then how changed the aspect; those rough, craggy sides which gave us so much pain and were so revolting to us, have become radiant with divine life and light and love. Opaque as they were to us when we went down, they have now become such a reflex of the Divine as to flash with the brilliancy of the diamond.

The place has become sweeter to us than any other can be, and we say,

Father, let me always stay here, hidden away from the strife of tongues, for the shadow of the cross is more grateful to me than anything else. The flowers are more fragrant and beautiful than elsewhere.

But after a little we are taken out from this sweet resting place, for God has a new field of labor for us. There are other hearts sorrowing who need just the lesson we have learned down in that sweet place, and we are chosen to help them. But we do not come up on the side where we made our descent. We went down on the side of suffering humanity, but we come up into the resurrected life of Christ as never before, and every remembrance of this sweet trysting-place is like liquid melody floating through the soul.

www.ingramcontent.com/pod-product-compliance
Lightning Source LLC
Chambersburg PA
CBHW032103010726
47493CB00008B/2506